Is A Worry Worrying You?

By Ferida Wolff and Harriet May Savitz
Illustrations By Marie Le Tourneau

Tanglewood • Indianapolis

Hardcover published by Tanglewood Publishing, Inc., May 2005.
Paperback published by Tanglewood Publishing, Inc., April 2007.

Design by Amy Alick Perich

Tanglewood Publishing, Inc.
1060 N. Capitol Ave., Ste. E-395
Indianapolis, IN 46204
www.tanglewoodbooks.com

Manufactured by LSC
Printed in the USA
10 9 8

Hardcover ISBN-10 0-9749303-2-6, ISBN-13 978-0-9749303-2-9
Paperback ISBN-10 1-933718-05-6, ISBN-13 978-1-933718-05-7

Library of Congress Cataloging in Publication Data

Wolff, Ferida; Savitz, Harriet May
  Is a worry worrying you? / by Ferida Wolff and Harriet May Savitz ; illustrations by Marie Letourneau.
p.   cm.
   Summary: Suggests creative and practical means to address worries, from a monster under the bed to a loud and frightening uncle.
   ISBN-10: 978-0-9749303-2-6
   ISBN-13: 978-0-9749303-2-9

[1. Worry—Fiction. 2. Problem solving—Fiction.] I. Marie Letourneau, ill. II. Title

PZ7.W82124 Is 2005
[E]—22

                2006277607

Do you ever have a worry that won't go away? What is a worry, anyway?

A worry is a thought that stops you from having fun, from feeling good, from being happy.

Don't bother looking for a worry because you'll never find it. It is invisible.
But it seems very real.

Suppose, just suppose, one hundred elephants come to tea and you discover you don't have any tea bags. Uh, oh. What will you do with a herd of thirsty elephants? Now, that's a worry!

But you can get rid of that worry by offering the elephants lemonade instead.

You can feel tired from a worry. Or sad. Or sick.
A worry can feel like a heavy sack is on your back. Only it isn't there.

Suppose a gorilla at the playground borrows your
skateboard and doesn't return it when he said he would.
You give yourself a stomachache because you are
sure that he will keep it forever.

Now, that's a worry.

But you can get rid of that worry by
going up to that gorilla and asking for it back.

Or maybe you can make a deal.

You borrow his roller blades
and the two of you can skate together.

A worry can scare you out of your shoes.

Suppose a monster moves in under your bed, and you're afraid if you go to sleep it will do something horrible, so you stay awake all night.

Now, that's a worry!

But you can get rid of that worry by singing the monster lullabies until you both fall asleep.

A worry can make a perfect day seem gloomy. Suppose you are all ready for the first day of school, but you find out that your new teacher is a bear. What will happen if you forget your homework? Now, that's a worry.

But you can get rid of that worry by thinking about how your teacher might feel in a new class. You give her a jar of honey to make her feel welcome.

Anyone can have a worry. Parents. Teachers. Brothers. Sisters. Friends.

Suppose Camille Camel, who is your best friend, is getting ready for a fancy party and falls and scrapes her knees. She is worried that she won't be able to go, so she comes to you for help but you don't know what to do. Now, both of you have a worry.

But you can get rid of both worries by putting bright pink bandages with yellow stars on her scraped knees. She smiles and goes off to the party while your worry disappears because you helped a friend.

A worry isn't polite. It has no manners.

It doesn't ask if it can enter. It just barges in.
And it will stay as long as you let it.

Suppose Uncle Herman is coming to visit, and you know he'll want to see you but his voice is as loud as a roaring lion, and it makes you want to run away. Now, that's a worry.

But you can get rid of that worry by remembering that you always have a good time with Uncle Herman because he likes to play board games with you, and he doesn't talk so much then. Get out your checkers. Here he comes.

Most of the time, something you worry about never happens. Suppose you see a rhinoceros walking on the other side of the street. He is so big and strong. What if he were to cross over and hit you! That is a worry.

But he is on his way to the store and never even looks at you.

A worry is as big or as small as you let it be.

Suppose a bald eagle makes a nest in your tangled hair, and you think everyone will laugh at you because you have an eagle on your head. Or worse, it will build a nest so big that you won't be able to get out of it. Or even worse than that, it will think you are a newborn eaglet and fly away with you and you will never see your family again!

Now, that's certainly a worry!
But you can stop that worry as soon as it gets started by getting a haircut.
The eagle will just have to find another tangle to build its nest.

So, how can you get rid of a worry once it starts worrying you? You can… Imagine it away. Put it in a suitcase and send it packing. Seal it in an envelope and mail it away.

Stand it in the corner while you have fun. Hide it in a closet and close the door.

Do something else. Take out your deck of cards and don't let it play.

Write a story. Play with a friend. Bake a cake.

Face it. Look at it and see if it makes any sense. Tell it to go away. Discuss your worry with someone else. Work on the thing that is worrying you.

Think another thought. Remember a good time that you had. Think about what you are doing and not about what might happen. Replace a worry with a happy thought. Let a worry thought remind you to smile.

A worry knows something that you should know: You can get rid of a worry
any time you want. It just takes a little patience. Don't worry. You can do it!